Ann Coburn has written extensively for the stage and TV and is the author of several novels for older children, including *Glint*, which won an Arts Council Writer's Award and a Northern Writer's Award, and The Borderlands Sequence, a quartet of novels that also won an Arts Council Writer's Award. Before becoming a full-time writer, Ann worked as an English teacher in an inner-city comprehensive school. She has given talks and run creative writing workshops for children and adults since her first novel was published in 1991. Ann lives in Northumberland.

You can find out more about Ariting her

Books by the same author

Dream Team Mission 1:
Flying Solo

Dream Team Mission 2:
Showtime

Dream Team Mission 3:
Speed Challenge

DreamTeam

"your dreams delivered"

Mission 4: The Daydream Shift

Ann Coburn

WALKER
BOOKS

First published 2007 by Walker Books Ltd
87 Vauxhall Walk, London SE11 5HJ

2 4 6 8 10 9 7 5 3 1

Text © 2007 Ann Coburn
Illustrations © 2007 Garry Parsons

The right of Ann Coburn and Garry Parsons to be identified
as author and illustrator respectively of this work has been
asserted by them in accordance with the Copyright, Designs
and Patents Act 1988

This book has been typeset in Stone Informal

Printed and bound in Great Britain by Creative Print and
Design (Wales), Ebbw Vale

British Library Cataloguing in Publication Data:
a catalogue record for this book is available
from the British Library

ISBN 978-1-84428-073-5

www.walkerbooks.co.uk

Contents

The Accidental	7
GOAL!	25
Train Surfing	61
Feeding Time	93
The Wasp Jar	131

The Accidental

Vert stood to attention in Team Leader Flint's office.

"At ease," said Team Leader Flint, without glancing up from her work.

"Yes, boss," said Vert. He tried to relax, but his back stayed as straight as a ruler, his arms remained stiffly at his sides and his feet appeared to be glued together. He could never be "at ease" in Team Leader

Flint's office. There were too many of
her personal things scattered around.
Looking at them made him blush.

A framed copy of the Three Abiding
Rules was hanging on the wall behind
Team Leader Flint's head. Vert tried to
keep his eyes focused on it, but his gaze
soon drifted down to the family photos

 on her desk. In one
shot she was, well …
laughing. Vert was
fascinated. It was
so strange and
unexpected – like
seeing a shark in
a party hat. He
leant down for a closer look.

"Come on, then," said Team Leader
Flint. "Let's hear it."

Vert snapped his head up so fast, his
neck clicked. "Pardon me?" he asked.

"Spit it out!"

Vert gulped. "Um… I think it's very nice. You look very – happy."

"What are you talking about?"

Vert pointed at the photograph. Team Leader Flint closed her eyes and pinched the bridge of her nose. "Mis-ter Vert," she sighed. "I am asking why you are here. Would you care to tell me?"

Vert felt his face turn bright red. The points of his ears tingled with embarrassment. "I have to report an Accidental," he squeaked.

"Then shall we get on with it?" said Team Leader Flint. She pulled an old leather-bound book from her shelf, slammed it down on her desk and flicked through pages filled with reports of previous Accidentals.

While he waited for Team Leader Flint to find her place, Vert glanced towards

the office door. Through the glass in
the top he could see Midge, Harley and
Snaffle, the other three members of his
dream team, waiting for him in the
corridor. Midge beamed at him. Harley
did a thumbs-up. Snaffle gave him a
curt nod.

Vert smiled. He could see how hard
it was for Snaffle not to sneer. He also
knew why Snaffle was making such an
effort. He, Snaffle, Midge and Harley
were all trainee Dream Fetchers,
learning how to deliver dreams to
humans. As part of their training, each
of them had to complete four Earthside

missions. During their third mission, the speed challenge, Vert had crashed his dreamskoot into a snowman. Midge and Harley had turned back to help him, but Snaffle had left them behind and raced back to Dreamside to win the speed challenge. Now he was trying to make amends and Vert appreciated the effort. He returned Snaffle's nod.

"Mis-ter Vert!"

Vert jumped and turned back to Team Leader Flint. She had found her place and was waiting, pen poised over the page. He cleared his throat and began his report. "The Accidental happened during my speed challenge. A nine-year-old human girl called Daisy came out into her garden and spotted me."

Team Leader Flint stopped writing and looked up. "Why didn't you hide?" she asked.

Vert hesitated. There had been nowhere to hide because he had been clinging to the side of a snowman at the time, but he could not tell Team Leader Flint that. She didn't know about his crash. "It all happened so fast," he said lamely.

"Hmmm." Team Leader Flint eyed him for a few seconds and then moved on. "Did the human child get a good look at you?"

"Yes," Vert admitted. "But she thought I was a fairy."

"Are you sure? Did she actually use –" Team Leader Flint shuddered and screwed up her face as though she had a bad taste in her mouth – "the 'F' word?"

Vert nodded. "She asked if I was a snow fairy."

"And?"

"And I said I was."

"Well done. That was good thinking.

Any other humans with her?"

"No, boss."

Team Leader Flint sat back and fixed Vert with a stare. "Only Daisy saw you? You're absolutely certain?"

"Yes, boss."

"You know why I'm asking, don't you," she said, pointing to her framed copy of the Three Abiding Rules.

Vert nodded.

"Read them out," Team Leader Flint insisted.

"Rule One. Always deliver what the customer orders. Rule Two. Don't look inside the box. Rule Three..." Vert stopped.

"Yes?"

"Rule Three. Never be seen," Vert whispered.

"The first two Abiding Rules protect our customers. Every human has the right to choose their own dreams and the right to keep those dreams private. The third Abiding Rule is for our protection. Without it, we would not survive. Humans are full of curiosity. If they ever suspect that we exist, they will not stop until they find Dreamside. And that will be the end of everything. Whenever a Dream Fetcher is careless enough to be seen by a human, he puts the whole of Dreamside at risk."

"I'm sorry," Vert gasped.

"Yes. Well. In your case, I think we can say it was a contained Accidental," said Team Leader Flint. She scribbled a few more words and signed her name with a flourish. "Try to be more careful in future. Dismissed."

Vert knew he was supposed to salute and leave the office. Instead, he stayed in front of Team Leader Flint's desk. He had something else to say, but he had to find the courage to begin.

"Don't look so worried," said Team Leader Flint. "Nobody likes to report an Accidental, but these things happen. And – well, just between you and me, a human catching sight of a Dream Fetcher is not always a bad thing. It can bring them on in leaps and bounds. Let me show you what I mean." She pulled another leather-bound book from the shelf. "See?" she said, opening the book. "This is an illustrated history of celebrated Accidentals."

"Oh! I know who he is," Vert said, spotting a portrait of a human in a velvet jerkin and a white ruff. "We learnt about him in Human Studies just last week. William Shakespeare."

"That's right. He's a famous Earthside writer from their sixteenth century."

"And he saw a Dream Fetcher?"

"Unfortunately, yes," said Team Leader Flint. "That's writers for you. Up at all hours of the night when they should be fast asleep. He went on to write a play about it, called *A Midsummer Night's Dream*."

"Shakespeare wrote about Dream Fetchers?"

"Not exactly." Team Leader Flint scowled. "He thought he'd seen a you-know-what –"

"Fairy?" Vert guessed.

Team Leader Flint shuddered. "Yes. That. But everyone in Dreamside knows it was a Dream Fetcher."

"And what about this one, boss?" asked Vert, pointing to a sketch of a female human who was sprinkling chopped tomatoes and grated cheese onto a round of bread dough.

"Ah, now. Have a look at what she's making. What does it remind you of?"

Vert knew the answer right away. His parents had been saving up to put him through Dream Fetcher training ever since he was a baby, but secretly he had always wanted to be a Dream Chef. He spent all his spare time in the Dream Kitchens, rolling out rounds of dream-dough ready for Motza, the Head Dream Chef, to add the correct blend of dream toppings for each order.

"That's the way we make dreams," he said.

"Exactly! This human is a very early example of a rare Double Accidental. Not only did she see a Dream Fetcher, but she also saw an actual dream – up close and out of the box."

Vert gasped. "How did that happen?"

"The Dream Fetcher panicked when his customer woke up. He tightened his grip on the dream box instead of letting go. The dream slid out of the box and his customer got a good look as it fell towards her. Of course, once the dream landed on her forehead she went back to sleep. But the very next day that human rolled out a circle of bread dough, added some toppings and baked it. She called it a 'pizza'. Humans all over Earthside are still eating pizza today. It's one of their most popular foods."

Team Leader Flint glanced at the time and then slammed the book shut.

"Off you go now," she said, turning back to her paperwork.

"Yes, boss," said Vert, staying right where he was.

Team Leader Flint lost her patience. "Vert! Get out! You have a lot to do. In case you've forgotten, you'll be flying your fourth and final training mission very soon."

Vert looked down at his feet. He could feel the points of his ears drooping. "No I won't," he said miserably.

"What?"

"I won't be flying the daydream shift." He took an envelope from his jacket and put it on the desk.

"What's this?" asked Team Leader Flint.

Vert straightened his shoulders and stood to attention. "My letter of resignation," he said. "I'm quitting, boss." His chin wobbled as he spoke.

He did not want to leave his dream team, but it had to be done.

Team Leader Flint did not seem surprised. She pointed to a chair beside her desk. "Sit down."

Vert hesitated. Nobody sat in the chair. Ever. Team Leader Flint always made her trainees stand.

"Sit!" Team Leader Flint snapped. Vert sat. A cloud of dust rose from the chair and settled onto his uniform. He tried to brush it away but only made things worse. *Never mind*, he thought sadly, looking down at the grey smudges on his uniform. *I won't need it much longer.*

"Now. Tell me why," said Team Leader Flint.

Vert took a deep breath and told her the secret he had been keeping ever since the start of his training. "I'm scared of flying."

"I know that!" said Team Leader Flint. "I've known since your very first dreamskoot flight."

Vert stared. He opened his mouth but no sound came out.

"There's always at least one trainee. Every year," Team Leader Flint continued. "You know Swift?"

Vert nodded. Everybody knew Swift. She was the best Dream Fetcher in their dream centre.

"Swift used to be scared of flying," said Team Leader Flint. "She kept going, though. I'd hoped you would too."

Vert shrugged and looked down at his boots.

"One more mission and you're fully qualified. Why give up now?"

"I can't tell you," said Vert.

"You won't get anyone into trouble. I promise."

"Well... It was during my speed challenge. I was so busy not looking down, I crashed into a snowman –"

"– and Midge and Harley came to rescue you," said Team Leader Flint. "Yes, yes, I know all about that too."

"Oh," said Vert. He was beginning to wonder if there was anything Team Leader Flint did not know.

"Totally against the rules, of course," said Team Leader Flint. "Midge and Harley should have called out Dreamside Search and Rescue. Instead they put themselves at risk. I'm very angry with them," said Team Leader Flint. But she didn't sound angry. She sounded rather proud.

"They didn't put themselves at risk,"

said Vert. "*I* put them at risk. I crashed because I'm scared of flying – and then they had to fly into a blizzard to rescue me! That's why I have to leave. I'm a danger to others."

"In that case, I'd better get rid of Midge, Harley and Snaffle too."

"Oh no! – I mean, why would you do that, boss?"

"They're a danger to others," said Team Leader Flint. "Harley flies dangerously fast. Midge is dangerously curious about Earthside and Snaffle is dangerously keen to win points."

"But—"

"But what, Vert?"

"But there's much more to them than that."

"Exactly! Harley would fight to the death for any one of you. Midge is brilliant in an emergency. Snaffle is a great navigator. And you, Vert – you have so much respect for the dreams you carry, you have never yet failed to make a delivery."

Vert blushed. He did not know what to say.

"You're not the danger, Vert. The danger is out there. That's why we put you into dream teams, so that you can look after each other. Are you going to let your dream team mates face the daydream shift without you? Well? Are you?"

Midge stood on tiptoe to peer through the window in Team Leader Flint's office door. "What's happening?" she asked. "Where's Vert gone?"

"He's still in there," said Snaffle. "But you're too short to see him now that he's sitting down."

Midge scowled up at Snaffle. She hated being small. Most Dream Fetchers were at least seven centimetres tall, but she was only six and three quarters – a shortcoming that Snaffle never let her forget. She was about to answer back when the rest of his sentence sank in. "Sitting down?" she said. "Vert is *sitting down*?"

"Is there an echo in here?" Snaffle remarked.

Midge turned her back on Snaffle and looked at Harley, who was propped against the wall with her eyes closed. Midge gazed at her admiringly. Harley could fall asleep just about anywhere. "Harley," she said. "Wake up."

Harley opened her eyes. "What?"

"Has Team Leader Flint ever let a trainee sit down in her office?" asked Midge.

"Unheard-of," said Harley.

"Until now," said Midge, nodding towards the office door.

Harley peered through the glass. "What's going on in there?"

"Vert must be in trouble," said Snaffle.

"You'd like that, wouldn't you?" Harley snapped.

Snaffle glared at Harley. "Oh dear. Still upset because I beat you in the speed challenge?"

"You didn't beat me!" Harley yelled. "I turned back. To help Vert!"

"Will you two stop shouting?" Midge begged.

"I would've won," Harley muttered.

"You wouldn't have."

"Would!"

"Wouldn't!"

"That is quite enough," said a voice behind them.

Midge, Snaffle and Harley all jumped to

attention. Team Leader Flint was standing in the corridor with Vert beside her. She froze them with an icy glare and then stalked off towards the Dream Centre without another word.

"That was your fault!" Snaffle hissed as they hurried after Team Leader Flint.

"No, it was your fault!" Harley retorted.

"No, yours!"

"Yours!"

Midge sighed. What was happening to her dream team? Ever since the speed challenge, Vert had been miserable and Harley and Snaffle had not stopped fighting. She left them to it and caught up with Vert. "What were you and Team Leader Flint talking about?" she asked.

Vert shrugged. "Just reporting my Accidental."

"It took ages! And you were sitting down."

"Yes."

"Are you all right?"

"Fine."

"Not in trouble, then?"

"No."

Midge studied Vert. Was he telling the truth? He was pale and the points of his ears were drooping, but there was nothing strange about that. Vert always looked ill on mission mornings. She wanted to ask more questions but they had reached the double doors at the end of the corridor. The Dream Centre was on the other side of those doors. Their fourth and final training mission was about to begin.

Midge smiled as she stepped into the Dream Centre. It was her favourite place in the whole of Dreamside. She stopped just inside the doors to take it all in. There was the Switchboard Room, where all incoming dream orders were logged. Next in line were the Dream Kitchens, where dreams were prepared, baked and boxed for delivery. The dreamskoot garages were at the far end of the row and the Dream Traffic Control Tower rose high above all the other buildings.

Midge's smile widened as she spotted lines of Dream Chefs marching from the kitchens, carrying freshly baked dreams to the launch pads. Soon she would be heading for Earthside with one of those orders on the back of her dreamskoot.

"No time to stop and smile, Midge!" Team Leader Flint snapped. "We don't want to miss our take-off slot. Stand by your dreamskoots. I'll be there shortly."

Team Leader Flint headed for the kitchens. Midge followed the other three towards the long line of launch pads

that stretched across the middle of the
Dream Centre.

Beyond the launch pads the floor fell
away and the ceiling rose, opening up a
space big enough to hold the gateway.
The gateway was set into the far wall of
the Dream Centre. It was a huge circular
frame filled with shimmering, changing
colours. This was the opening between
Dreamside and Earthside.
Dreamskoots were constantly
passing through it, carrying
dreams to Earthside or
returning to base.

Midge caught up with the rest of her dream team on the metal walkway behind their launch pads. She would have liked to lean against the railing and watch the gateway traffic while she waited for Team Leader Flint, but Harley was shouting at Snaffle again.

Midge sighed. "What's the matter now?"

"He's hiding something!" Harley yelled. "Show me!"

Snaffle had his hands behind his back. "It's not for you. It's for Vert."

"Then why don't you give it to him?" Midge asked.

"She won't let me," Snaffle snarled, glaring at Harley.

"I want to see it first!" Harley shouted. "Knowing him, it'll be something horrible."

"I wish you'd stop!" Midge cried.

"We're supposed to be a dream team. We're supposed to look out for one another."

"I am!" Harley retorted. "I'm looking out for Vert."

"What does Vert think about that?" Midge asked.

Harley and Snaffle both looked at Midge, then at one another and, finally, at Vert.

"I think," Vert said, "I think I'd like to see what Snaffle has for me."

Harley tutted. Snaffle gave her a smug look and handed Vert a small package.

Vert tore away the tissue-paper wrapping. "Flying goggles. Thank you," he said politely.

"Not just ordinary goggles," Snaffle explained. "If you use them, you won't be scared of flying any more."

"Huh!" Harley sniffed.

"Snaffle," Midge scolded. "You shouldn't say things like that."

"No, really!" said Snaffle. "I had those goggles specially made, Vert. See the little button on the side there? If you press it when you're in the air, the goggles will make it look as though there's a solid road under your dreamskoot. Whichever way you turn, the road will be there in front of you."

Vert smiled. The points of his ears perked up. "Thank you, Snaffle," he whispered, clutching the goggles to his chest. "Thank you."

Harley saw the relief on Vert's face. She grinned. "Well. That's all right then," she said, giving Snaffle a hug. Snaffle scowled but his cheeks turned pink with pleasure.

Midge smiled. They were a dream team again. And just in time. Team Leader Flint was heading their way.

"Listen up!" Team Leader Flint ordered as soon as her boots hit the walkway. "We don't have much time. As you know, before you can

graduate you must complete one final mission – the daydream shift. So far you have delivered your dream orders under cover of darkness. Today you will be flying in full daylight when most humans, apart from the dreamers, are awake and alert."

Team Leader Flint paused and looked at each one of them in turn. "Make no mistake," she continued. "Daydream delivery can be dangerous. You need to have your wits about you. Understood?"

"Yes, boss," they chorused.

"I've just had a word with Motza – I mean Signore Mozzarella. He will be hand-picking four of the easiest deliveries for you," said Team Leader Flint. She pointed to the Dream Kitchens. Motza, the Head Dream Chef, was standing in the doorway. He grinned and gave them a double thumbs-up

before heading
back into the steamy
kitchens.

"You shouldn't have
any problems," Team
Leader Flint continued.
"But Dreamside
Search and Rescue are
on full alert, just in case." She pointed
over at Cheroot, Head of Search and
Rescue. He did not look very alert. He
was lounging against his skoot and
chewing on an unlit cigar.

"Cool," breathed Harley.

"Hmmm," said Team Leader Flint.
"Moving on. You will fly each mission in
pairs for extra safety. Midge and Harley,
you are flying first. Midge, Vert will ride
with you. Harley, you take Snaffle. Any
questions? Any – complaints?"

Team Leader Flint gave them each a

hard look. Midge held her breath but she need not have worried. Harley draped an arm around Snaffle's shoulders, Snaffle managed not to sneer and Vert, still clutching his new goggles, smiled. The Dream Team was together and ready for action.

"No complaints, boss," said Midge.

"Good," said Team Leader Flint, making a note on her clipboard. "Now where are those deliveries?"

They all scanned the crowds between the launch pads and the Dream Kitchens, trying to spot a bobbing chef's hat heading their way. Midge went up on tiptoe to get a better view. As she did, the metal walkway panel shifted under her feet. Midge lost her balance, stumbled back onto her heels and looked down. A shock of fear ran through her.

Something was down there!

Something was
wedged into the crawl
space under the
walkway panel. It
was glaring up
at her through
the metal mesh.
Its eyes
gleamed red.

Midge felt her
breath catch in
her throat. The thing
under the walkway hated her. She could
see the hatred in those gleaming red eyes.
She could feel it, rising through the mesh
in icy waves. She jumped away onto the
next walkway panel. Too frightened to
speak, she turned to Harley and reached
for her arm.

"There!" Harley yelled, pointing.

Midge gasped and spun around,

expecting to see the red-eyed creature climbing out onto the walkway. Instead she saw a Dream Chef pushing through the crowds, carrying two dream boxes above his head.

"Our deliveries!" said Harley.

Midge forced herself to look down again. There were still two red dots under the walkway panel, but now she could see that they were only the reflections of launch-pad landing lights. She bent closer and peered through the mesh. The crawl space below her was empty, but she thought she heard a faint *skreeee* from the darkness beyond. It sounded like sharp claws scraping across metal.

"To your dreamskoots!" ordered Team Leader Flint.

Midge shook herself and straightened up. This was no time to be imagining monsters. She had a mission to complete. She hurried to the launch pads after Harley. They both climbed onto their dreamskoots and Vert and Snaffle climbed on behind them. Midge felt her dreamskoot shudder as the chef slotted a dream box into the holder. She turned to Vert.

"Ready?" she asked.

Vert settled his new goggles over his eyes. "Ready," he said, putting his arms around her waist.

Midge looked across at Harley's launch pad. "Take care out there!"

Harley grinned. "Hey!" she yelled back. "How hard can it be?"

Her voice floated down from the

launch pads and echoed around the crawl space under the walkway.

How hard can it be..? How hard ... hard ... hard...?

Something shifted in the darkness as it listened to Harley's words. "Much harder than you think," was the hissed reply. "The Dream Team is about to have a very bad day."

Nobody heard the voice in the crawl space below them, and nobody noticed a sound like sharp claws against metal as the shape skittered away.

Skree ... skree ... skree...

The sound faded, lost in the noise and bustle of the Dream Centre. Up on the launch pads, Midge had already forgotten her fright. She was too busy preparing to launch. "Lift off!" she ordered, gripping her handlebars.

Her dreamskoot rose into the air.

"Wings out!" Two silvery wings opened out from beneath the footplates.

"Earthside!" Midge and Harley yelled together.

Their dreamskoots shot forward. Midge held her breath as she passed through the gateway. She could never quite get used to the feeling of being dragged through warm jelly. A second later she burst through into Earthside.

"Wow!" she gasped. She was used to seeing Earthside at night, when the only colours were silvery moonlight and the yellow glow of streetlights. In daylight the sky was a bright, clear blue. The rooftops of the town below were a warm red. Sunlight danced on the sea and made the river sparkle.

"Whoo-hoo!" Harley yelled, zipping past Midge. In no time at all she was just a dot in the sky.

Midge spoke into her helmet dreamcom. "Vert? I need to get moving now. Are your new goggles working?"

"Oh yes," said Vert happily. "Go as fast as you like."

Midge opened up the throttle and set off at top speed. "The daydream is for a customer called George," she said, reading the details off the screen. "He's at a football ground."

"Funny place to fall asleep," said Vert.

"He's probably just finished cutting the grass or something."

"Having a lunchtime nap," Vert agreed.

"There it is, dead ahead." The football ground was right on the edge of town, with only fields beyond. Midge gave a satisfied nod. There was not a single human in sight. The daydream shift was turning out to be her easiest mission of all. She flew in low across the fields,

dodging from hedgerow to hedgerow until she reached the back fence of the football ground. It was a very high fence. Midge brought her dreamskoot to a halt and gazed upwards. She could just see the roof of the stands poking above the fence.

"Vert? How are you doing? Are those goggles still working?"

"We're on a tarmac road," said Vert happily. "With white lines down the middle. But I could have concrete if I wanted. Or a dirt track. Or – ooh! Guess what? I can even choose the colour!"

Midge smiled. "That's good, Vert. I'm going over the fence now." She left the safety of the hedgerow and flew upwards.

ROOAAARRGGHH!!!

Midge screeched to a stop, turned in mid-air and shot back under the hedge.

"Wh-what was that?" Vert stammered.

"Something big," said Midge. "With a very loud roar." She tried to come up with a list of big Earthside creatures with loud roars. Dinosaur? Wrong time. Lion? Wrong place. Bear? Gorilla? Elephant? Midge dismissed them all. What could it be? "Well we can't sit under this hedge all day," she said firmly. "I'm going to take a look." She edged her dreamskoot forward. She could hear Vert muttering into the earpiece of her dreamcom.

"Oh dear, oh my, oh dear me."

"Hush, Vert."

"Sorry."

Midge peered out between the branches. There was nothing in the field. There was nothing in the sky. She eased out from under the hedge and shot straight up into the air. Once she was high enough to be out of danger, she turned her dreamskoot in a tight circle, scanning the whole area.

"Whatever it was, it's gone," Vert said.

"Back to business, then." Midge began to climb towards the top of the fence.

ROOAAARRGGHH!!!

"Dive!" Vert screamed, grabbing her around the waist and holding on tight. Midge stayed where she was. "No need," she said in a trembling voice.

"I've just realized what it is."

"You have? What?"

"I'll show you." Midge eased her dreamskoot over the top of the fence and hovered there, looking down at the scene below. The football ground was full of humans. Two teams were running around on the pitch. One team was wearing tops of black and gold. The other team wore blue and white. The rest of the humans were all packed into the stands, watching the game.

"I thought this was meant to be an easy delivery," Vert gasped. "I thought the football ground would be empty."

"Me too," Midge sighed. "For once I wish I was Velvet."

Velvet and Midge were unlikely friends. Velvet also came from Dreamside, but she was a Collector. Collectors lived deep underground in The Below. They had

their own gateways through to Earthside and they worked in a vast network of tunnels. Their job was to supply the Dream Kitchens with human feelings, the raw ingredients for dream toppings. They had collecting caverns under all the places where humans gathered to share strong feelings. Midge knew that there was probably a collecting cavern under the football ground. Collectors would be down there now, harvesting all the hope and joy and anger that came seeping down through the pitch and into their collecting carts. Usually Midge hated the thought of living and working underground but, as she looked down at the seething crowds of humans below her, she would have been happy to trade places with Velvet.

Just then, a blue and white player knocked a black and gold player to the ground.

ROOAAARRGGHH!!

In the stands, the humans with the black and gold scarves shook their fists. They looked furious. Midge gulped.

"We can't go down there," Vert whimpered. "Look at them!"

"One step at a time," Midge said. "First, let's find out where George is." She pressed a button and a plan of the football ground appeared on her map screen. There was a flashing red dot on the plan. It was right in the middle of the stand full of angry humans.

"How can anyone be sleeping down there?" Vert said.

Midge scanned the crowd, trying to spot a sleeping human. They all looked horribly wide awake. "He's in that stand somewhere," she said, pointing at the red dot on her screen. "I'd better go over for a closer look."

"Are you kidding?" Vert squeaked. "Abiding Rule Number Three. *Never be seen.*"

"Yes, but humans hardly ever look up, especially the older ones. Even when they do, they're usually thinking about other things. Grown-up humans never notice anything," said Midge, trying to sound braver than she felt. "We just need to wait until they're concentrating on something else."

"Like now?" Vert asked.

Midge looked down. The black and gold footballer had picked himself up. He was standing with the ball at his feet, facing a big net. Four of the blue and white players were lining up in front of the net. A very tall human wearing huge gloves was telling them exactly where to stand. The crowd had gone quiet. They were all watching the pitch.

"Yes," said Midge. "Like now." She urged her dreamskoot forward and skimmed over the heads of the crowd. Below her, the human with the huge gloves stepped back into the net and spread out his arms. Everything went very still. The whole crowd was looking at the black and gold footballer with the ball at his feet. Midge nodded. It was just as she thought. The humans were too busy watching the game to notice a tiny dreamskoot flying overhead.

BLAM!

Midge gasped at the sudden loud noise. Then she gasped again. Every single human was suddenly looking at her! No. They were looking at –

"The ball!" Vert yelled.

It was flying towards them with all the force of the footballer's kick behind it.

Midge put her dreamskoot into a steep dive. The ball flew past, close enough for her to see every stitch in the leather and catch the smell of grass and mud.

"Human!" Vert screamed. Midge snapped her head around. The tall human with the huge gloves was jumping up towards the ball

– and Midge
was heading straight
for his face. She yanked
back on the handlebars. Her
dreamskoot groaned and shuddered
and then finally
began to turn.
The human
had been
about to
catch the
ball but,
as Midge
scraped

past his nose, he blinked. The ball flew under his arm and into the big net.

ROOAAARRGGHH!!!

Midge shot into the gap under the stands and landed in the dirt. Above them, the crowd was going crazy. Midge and Vert clung to one another as hundreds of boots thundered over their heads. They looked out at the pitch. The human with the huge gloves was scratching his head and looking up at the sky. All the black and gold footballers were running around and jumping on one another.

"I think we just helped the home team to score a goal," Midge gasped.

Out on the pitch, the black and gold players spread their arms out like wings and ran up and down in front of their fans.

"Oh no!" Vert said. "They must have seen us!"

"I don't think so," Midge said.

"But look! They're pretending to fly!"

"I know, but I don't think they're pretending to be us," Midge said,

watching the footballers. "They've done this before. See how they're all moving together and turning at the same time? It's a sort of dance. A celebration dance."

"That's a relief," Vert said, remembering what Team Leader Flint had said about the consequences of being seen. "So. What now?"

Midge looked at the red dot on her screen. Her shoulders slumped. "I think I'll have to give up on this mission. I can't go out there again. I'm too scared."

"Maybe you won't have to," Vert said softly.

"What do you mean?" asked Midge, turning to face him.

Vert pointed to the space under the back of the stand. Midge turned to look. A white van was parked there.

"Look at the sign on the side," Vert said.

"George's Ices," Midge read.

"And look through those big windows."

Midge looked. Inside the van, a human was slumped on a stool in front of a bench with his head resting on his arms. He was fast asleep. "George," she breathed. "He wasn't in the stand. He was under it! Pass me that daydream, Vert."

"He won't sell many ice creams under here," Vert said as Midge flew towards the open window in the side of the van.

"He will at the end of the match. All those humans will come pouring off the terraces, right past this van," Midge said.

"Quick! Make the dream-drop and let's get out of here!" Vert hissed, looking over his shoulder.

"Here goes." Midge grasped the box and flew in through the open window of the ice-cream van. She swooped down and let go of the dream. The box landed neatly on the back of George's head.

Phut!

The dream disappeared. Midge had completed her delivery. With a sigh of relief she flew out of the van, nipped over the fence behind the stand and set her course back to Dreamside.

"If that was meant to be an easy daydream delivery, I'd hate to try a difficult one," said Vert.

"I know," Midge agreed. "I hope Harley isn't taking too many risks out there."

Train Surfing

Harley sped across the roof of the town hall on her dreamskoot. She was heading straight for the bell tower. At the very last second, she kinked to the left and then shot skywards, narrowly missing the spinning weathervane on top of the tower.

"Whooo-hooo!" she yelled. "That was fun!"

"Harley," Snaffle said into his dreamcom.

"Did you see how I timed it just right?"

"Harley."

"Let's go to the beach next."

"Harley!" Snaffle yelled, knocking his fist against the back of her helmet.

"Oww!"

"In case you'd forgotten," Snaffle snapped, "we are Earthside. In daylight. In full view of all those humans down in the high street."

Harley snorted. "Huh! Those humans won't notice us. They're too busy shopping."

"And another thing," Snaffle continued. "Your daydream order is getting colder by the second, and you haven't even checked your delivery details yet!"

Harley sighed. Snaffle was right. "Sorry," she said, landing on a quiet rooftop. "Earthside is just so amazing in daylight. I'll check my screen right now."

"About time," Snaffle muttered. "Honestly. If we're all going to graduate together..."

"We?" Harley turned around and grinned at Snaffle. "Did you say 'we'? Awww, Snaffle! I knew it. You do care about your dream team!"

Snaffle scowled and folded his arms. "I just don't want to be held back by the rest of you."

"You could always join another team," Harley teased.

"What? And end up with an even bigger bunch of idiots?"

"Seriously, though," said Harley. "That was a good thing you did, getting those special goggles for Vert. It was – I don't know – nice."

"Nice had nothing to do with it," Snaffle huffed. "I don't want to fly with someone who's too scared to open his eyes. I could get hurt."

Harley grinned. "You don't fool me," she said, giving him an affectionate punch on the shoulder.

"Can we get back to your delivery details?" Snaffle said.

Harley looked at the screen on her control panel. "The customer is an elderly female. Her name is Gertrude. Her location is... Rats! Hang on, Snaffle!"

Harley left the rooftop and shot up into the sky. She didn't stop until she was high enough to see the whole town spread out below her.

"What are you playing at?" Snaffle gasped.

"I need to see where the train is," Harley said.

"What train?"

Harley pointed.

"That one just coming into town. Gertrude is on it. I have to get to the station double-quick." She shot back down to chimney level and zoomed off across the rooftops. If she wanted to catch Gertrude's train, she would have to fly like the wind. Harley grinned as she coaxed more speed from her dreamskoot. There was nothing she liked better!

"I don't get it," Snaffle said as they leant into a tight turn around a chimney pot. "How are you supposed to deliver a daydream to this human? If she's getting off at the station, she'll be wide awake."

"Who says she's getting off the train?" Harley said.

"What do you mean?"

"Gertrude is fast asleep in the last carriage. That's why I need to be ready and waiting at the station when the train arrives. I have to sneak on board while the train doors are open, make my dream-drop and then get off again before the doors close."

"What? That's impossible!"

"Not impossible," Harley said as she cornered a church spire. "The humans will be so busy sorting out themselves and their luggage, they probably won't notice us."

"Probably?" Snaffle sighed into her earpiece. "What happened to those easy deliveries Motza was supposed to be picking out for our first daydream shift?"

"This one will be easy-peasy."

"You'll never know," Snaffle muttered, "because you're going to miss the train."

"No, I won't," Harley retorted, pointing out the station at the top of the hill. "We're nearly there, see?"

"That was fast," said Snaffle grudgingly. "You're not a bad navigator. For a girl."

"So kind," Harley drawled, deciding not to tell Snaffle that she already knew the way to the station. Early in her training, her friend Dare had shown her how easy it was to slip through the gateway when the Dream Centre was busy and nobody had the time to notice one more dreamskoot taking off. Since then she had been nipping through to Earthside to put in extra flying practice. One night she had met up with Dare and he had taken her train surfing. Harley grinned as she remembered.

What a thrill! As each train had left the station, she and Dare had landed their dreamskoots on the roof above the driver's cabin. The train had slowly picked up speed as it crossed the railway bridge. They had surfed it for as long as they could before the wind lifted them from the roof and sent their dreamskoots spiralling down towards the river below.

Harley reached the ruined castle next to the station and took cover behind a crumbling wall. She and Dare had perched there between trains. There was no time to perch now. Her customer's train was already pulling into the station. "Here goes," she said. She flew out from behind the castle wall and turned her dreamskoot towards the station.

"Stop!" Snaffle cried.

Harley shot back behind the wall. "What's the matter?" she asked.

"Too many humans," Snaffle said.

Harley looked around the empty ruin. "Where?"

"In the train carriage," Snaffle said. "On the platform. Didn't you see them?"

"Don't worry," Harley said. "There are loads of hiding places on trains."

"But Earthside is so bright in the daytime. We're bound to be spotted."

"It'll be fine."

"No, it won't," Snaffle said. "Something's wrong, Harley. You shouldn't have been given this delivery. It's a job for the most advanced Dream Fetchers

– experts in camouflage and disguise. You're only a trainee. Remember the Dream Fetcher's motto: *Makes you shiver? Don't deliver.*"

Harley hesitated. It was true. The delivery was a tricky one. But Motza, the Head Dream Chef, had picked it out especially for her. He must have thought she could do it. "It's my delivery," she decided. "So it's my call. I'm going for it."

"Please don't," Snaffle whispered. "I'm scared."

Harley looked around at Snaffle. He was pale and trembling. She looked back at the train. It was coming to a stop. Soon the carriage doors would be opening. She bit her lip. She hated the thought of turning back to Dreamside with a failed delivery, especially when

she knew she could do it, but Snaffle
was her team mate. He had swallowed
his pride and admitted that he was
frightened. Surely she could swallow her
pride too? "You know what, Snaffle?" she
said. "You're right. This delivery is too
risky. Let's go get another one."

Snaffle said nothing, but Harley knew
he was relieved. She felt him relax into
the saddle behind her. As she turned
her dreamskoot away from the station,
a shadow moved across the sun. Harley
shivered and looked up. Shock sizzled
through her. A huge white bird with
fierce yellow-rimmed eyes was staring
down at them. Behind her, Snaffle
gasped and tightened his grip around
her waist. She yanked her dreamskoot
over to one side. The bird swooped after
them. Harley held her course until the
bird was so close she could hear the

rush of wind through its feathers.

"Hang on, Snaffle!" she yelled, pulling up on her handlebars. Her dreamskoot shot skywards.

Clack!

The bird tried to grab the wing of her dreamskoot but its sharp beak snapped shut on thin air.

"Black-backed gull!" Snaffle cried as the huge bird flew past just below their feet. "We're in trouble."

Harley nodded grimly. She did not need to be told. The gull had already turned and was coming back for another attack. It opened its beak and screamed at them.

Kark! Kark! Kark!

The noise was so loud, it made Harley's helmet rattle. She put her dreamskoot into a steep dive.

Clack!

This time the beak snapped shut just above their heads. Harley brought her dreamskoot out of the dive and looked back. The gull had already banked around and was swooping towards them again. A chill ran through her. She could make her dreamskoot fly like an arrow, but this bird was faster. If she stayed in the air, the razor-sharp beak wouldn't miss a third time.

"Hang on, Snaffle!" she yelled. "I'm going for cover!"

As the gull closed in, Harley flew her dreamskoot straight at the crumbling castle wall.

"Pull up! We're going to crash!" Snaffle cried.

Harley kept going towards the wall. She was looking for the spot she and Dare had used as a shelter on the night they had gone train surfing.

Kark!

The gull was right on her tail. The stones loomed up in front of her. Desperately Harley searched the top of the wall. There it was! A narrow slit between two stones. She zipped towards it and steered into the gap. Her dreamskoot skidded through the dust, heading straight for the opening on the far side of the wall. In another second they would be back outside again.

"Brake!" she screamed.

Her dreamskoot stopped instantly. Snaffle cannoned into her back and squashed her against the control panel.

"Sorry," Snaffle muttered, shuffling backwards.

"It's OK," Harley replied automatically. Her voice was shaking. She sat up and checked her dreamskoot for damage. The little machine did not have a single scratch. Even the delicate wings were unharmed. They fluttered gently, keeping the dreamskoot in place as it hovered just inside the opening. Harley sighed with relief.

"Expert flying or what?" she boasted.

"Stupid and dangerous, that's what," Snaffle retorted.

"You're welcome," Harley said, lifting her helmet visor. From her perch inside the castle wall she could see the train. Nearly all the humans from the station platform had climbed on board. Carriage doors were beginning to slam shut. Harley looked at the last carriage.

She could see
Gertrude sitting
by the window,
fast asleep. Her
hands were
folded neatly

together across her chest. Her glasses had slid down her nose. Harley felt a twinge of regret that she would not be delivering Gertrude's daydream. For a few seconds she sat quietly in the dusty darkness, listening to the cries of the gull as it circled above the wall.

"We'll just have to wait here until it's gone," she said.

"What is it with me and birds?" Snaffle grumbled.

Harley gave a snort of laughter.

"It's not funny!" Snaffle said. "First the owl. Then the chickens. Now a great big gull!"

Harley snorted again. She put a hand over her mouth but that only made things worse. A strangled quack of laughter came from between her fingers. Snaffle sniggered behind her. Then he spluttered. Then he snorted too. Soon they were both laughing so hard they could not speak. They leant together, shaking their heads at one another to stop.

BOOM!

Suddenly Harley wasn't laughing any more. Dust and pieces of stone rained down onto her helmet. She lowered her visor and looked up. A hole had appeared in the crumbling mortar above their heads. A fierce yellow-rimmed eye glared down through the hole. The gull was on the top of the wall.

"Why won't it leave us alone?" Snaffle cried. "There must be tastier food out there!"

"I think this must be its patch," Harley said. "And we're trespassing."

BOOM!

The gull punched down through the mortar again. It drove its beak into the narrow shelter directly in front of Harley's face.

"We have to get out of here!" she yelled as the gull pulled back, leaving an even bigger hole.

"We can't!" Snaffle cried. "It'll catch us if we go outside."

"Well if we stay here, we'll be speared."

Harley looked out at the train. It was starting to move. She looked more closely at the last carriage. The sliding window in the carriage door was not quite shut. "Hold on, Snaffle!" she cried.

Snaffle grabbed onto her waist. Harley looked up. She had to time this perfectly. Through the hole she saw the gull pull back its head a third time. Harley opened up the throttle. Her dreamskoot shot out of the wall just as the gull broke through the last of the mortar. The sharp beak speared the floor where, an instant earlier, Snaffle had been sitting.

"Go! Go! Go!" Snaffle yelled.

Harley shot towards the train.

"Stop! Stop! Stop!" Snaffle cried, when he saw where she was heading.

Harley turned so that she was alongside the door of the last carriage. She flew beside the slowly moving train.

KARK! The gull swooped towards them.

Harley eyed the open window, judging speed and angles. She had spent hours on the Dreamside obstacle course, practising for a time like this.

"No! No! No!" Snaffle cried, as he realized what she was about to do.

Harley took one last look at the gull. It was nearly on top of them. "You lose, you big bully," she said, hopping neatly through the open window and into the train. The gull almost crashed into the door. Its big webbed feet

scraped against the glass as it veered away from the train. Harley didn't have time to watch it fly off into the sky. She was already searching for a hiding place.

They were in a little corridor between the carriages. She looked around. There were doors everywhere. Any one of them could open at any second. She flew down to a seat that was folded away into the wall and squeezed into the little space behind it.

"How about that?" she said, grinning round at Snaffle.

"Not very clever," Snaffle said. "Out of the frying pan into the fire if you ask me."

"You're welcome," Harley replied.

"And just how are you planning to get off a moving train?" Snaffle asked.

"Easy-peasy," Harley said. "I know how these trains work. They always go really slowly until they've crossed the railway bridge. Once we're sure the gull has gone, we can just hop out of the window again."

"Oh! Of course! And if that isn't dangerous enough for you, you could always deliver that daydream while we're here," muttered Snaffle.

Harley scowled. She knew Snaffle was only being nasty because he was scared, but she was starting to get annoyed. "Come to think of it," she retorted, "I might as well."

Just at that moment, the door to the end carriage slid open and a human stepped out. Before she could change her mind, Harley zipped through the doorway and into the carriage. Snaffle gave a little squeak of panic and then fell silent. Harley shot up into the luggage rack and hovered there while she checked out the carriage. It was full of humans.

She gulped. She could see Gertrude, still fast asleep in her seat, about halfway down the carriage. How was she going to reach her customer without being seen? She looked at the other passengers. Some of them were gazing out of the window. Some of them were reading. Quite a lot of them had little white boxes with wires leading up to their ears. The boxes were making a *tchkka*, *tchkka*, *tchkka* noise and the humans were nodding their heads to the beat.

Harley relaxed. The humans were all in their own little worlds. They were taking no notice of anything around them. Silently she floated down to floor level and began to make her way towards Gertrude under the seats.

"It stinks down here!" Snaffle hissed into her earpiece.

Harley wrinkled her nose. She had to

agree. A lot of the humans had taken
their shoes off. As she flew over a pair of
very smelly trainers, the owner jerked his
foot under the seat towards them. Harley
dodged the foot and flew straight inside
one of the trainers.

"Oh! Gross!" Snaffle whispered.

Harley was too busy holding her
breath to answer. The foot hooked the
other trainer out from under the seat.
Harley backed out of the remaining
trainer and shot back up to the luggage

rack. A second later a coat was pushed towards them.

"Umphh!" Snaffle said as they were squashed against the wall.

Harley backed her dreamskoot out from under the coat and ducked behind a handbag. The owner of the smelly trainers was standing up right next to them! Luckily he was looking towards the door at the other end of the carriage. Harley studied him. He was young and pale, with lots of studs and earrings. His long black hair had been moulded into enormous stiff spikes that stuck out all over his head. Harley looked at the spikes and smiled. "Hey, Snaffle," she whispered. "Remember what you said about camouflage?"

"Ye-es," Snaffle said warily.

"Watch this," said Harley. As the pale young human set off down the aisle,

Harley nipped out of the luggage rack
and lowered her dreamskoot into the
middle of his spiky hair. The human
didn't notice. He lumbered on towards
Gertrude with Harley and Snaffle safely
hidden in his spikes. "Pass me that
daydream," whispered
Harley.

As the human walked past Gertrude,
Harley flung the daydream towards her.
Not one human noticed the tiny dream
box come flying out of the young man's

hair. It landed on Gertrude's shoulder and disappeared.

Phut!

Harley gave Snaffle a thumbs-up.

Swishhh!

The door at the end of the carriage slid open and the spiky haired human stepped through. Harley rose out of his hair just before he disappeared into the next carriage. She looked at the train doors and grinned. "We're in luck," she said. "Someone's left this window open too."

Harley looked out. There was no sign of the gull. "Snaffle, we have to leave now, before the train picks up speed," she said. "Just to warn you, we're going to be flung about all over the place."

"Flung about?" Snaffle cried. "Flung where?"

"Don't worry. I know what I'm doing." Harley tried to sound more confident than she felt. She was not lying, exactly. She was good at train surfing, but up on the roof it had been easy to judge the wind. Today was different. She was about to fly from the train with no idea of how strong the wind outside would be. She took a deep breath. "Hang on, Snaffle. We're going train surfing!"

"OK," Snaffle said weakly, clamping his arms around her waist.

A fierce wind grabbed hold of Harley's dreamskoot as soon as she slipped out of the window. She did not fight it. She wanted to keep her dreamskoot wings in one piece. The wind snatched them away from the train, twirled them around a few times and then sent them spinning over the side of the railway bridge. Still, Harley did not fight it. She let her dreamskoot spiral down towards the river until she was sure the wind had let go. Only then

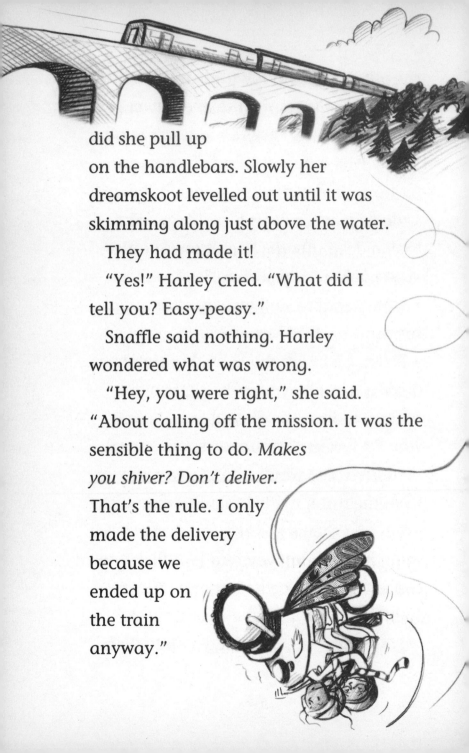

did she pull up
on the handlebars. Slowly her
dreamskoot levelled out until it was
skimming along just above the water.

They had made it!

"Yes!" Harley cried. "What did I
tell you? Easy-peasy."

Snaffle said nothing. Harley
wondered what was wrong.

"Hey, you were right," she said.
"About calling off the mission. It was the
sensible thing to do. *Makes
you shiver? Don't deliver.*
That's the rule. I only
made the delivery
because we
ended up on
the train
anyway."

Snaffle was silent.

Harley tried again. "I won't tell. About you being scared. Anyone would've been."

"*You* weren't," Snaffle said.

"Yeah, but I'm crazy!"

"True," Snaffle agreed, but with none of his usual energy.

Harley couldn't figure out what was wrong. "We did it, Snaffle!" she cried, trying to boost his spirits. "We survived our first daydream shift!"

"I still have mine to do," Snaffle said, with a quaver in his voice.

Finally Harley understood what was troubling Snaffle. "Your daydream delivery won't be like this one," she soothed. "The gull was just bad luck. And you'll have Midge riding pillion. She'll look after you."

"Unlike you," Snaffle muttered.

"What do you mean?"

"Weathervane charging. Gull dodging. Train surfing..."

Harley sighed. "All right. Get it over with. Say what you want to say. I'm a crazy flier. I have no proper fear. I'm stupid and dangerous."

"All of those," Snaffle said. "But," he added reluctantly, "the truth is, if I'd been flying, we'd be inside that gull's stomach by now. So. Um..."

"Thanks?" Harley suggested.

"Yes. That," Snaffle muttered.

Harley sent her dreamskoot dancing over the sparkling water. "You're welcome!" she sang.

Feeding Time

Team Leader Flint marched through the Dream Centre crowds. She was heading for the metal walkway behind the launch pads, where Midge, Vert, Harley and Snaffle were waiting for her. They were halfway through their fourth and final test: the daydream shift. Midge and Harley had already completed their missions. Now it was Vert and Snaffle's turn. As soon as Team

Leader Flint stepped onto the walkway, her four trainees came to attention and saluted. She slotted her clipboard under one arm and saluted in return.

"Listen up, trainees!" she barked. "This is no time for daydreaming!" She paused, expecting them to laugh. Her trainees were silent. She tried again. "I said, the daydream shift is no time for daydreaming..."

This time they managed four dutiful smiles, which quickly faded. Team Leader Flint raised her eyebrows. She had taken many dream teams through their training. She always gave them her "no-time-for-daydreaming" line halfway through their final mission. It wasn't very funny but they never failed to laugh. They laughed with sheer surprise that she had made a joke. They laughed with pleasure because the end of their training was in sight. They always laughed. Until now.

She studied her trainees more closely. Snaffle's hands were shaking. The points of Vert's ears were drooping badly. Midge kept bobbing up onto her toes to watch the chefs bringing fresh daydream deliveries from the kitchens. Even Harley was showing signs of nerves. She kept reaching up to touch the old neckerchief that had once belonged to her mother.

Team Leader Flint frowned. It made no sense. Vert was always a nervous wreck before a mission, but the other three ought to be feeling relaxed and happy after Midge and Harley's deliveries. They had been given the easiest orders Motza could find. He had chosen a night-shift worker sleeping alone in her house and a toddler taking a nap in his buggy in a quiet garden. Team Leader Flint had been leading a new trainee dream team around the obstacle course that morning, but she had been in constant radio contact with the Dream Traffic Control Centre. There had been no reported problems with Midge and Harley's missions. But the Control Centre screens could only track flight paths, they did not tell the whole story.

"Anything I need to know?" asked Team Leader Flint, looking at their worried faces.

Midge, Snaffle, Harley and Vert glanced

at one another then faced forwards again. "No, boss," they chorused.

Team Leader Flint sighed. They were keeping something from her, but at least they were doing it together. Finally they were working as a team. She decided to move on. "Very well," she said. "Vert and Snaffle, your daydream orders will be here any minute. You should have nothing to worry about with these deliveries. Motza has promised they'll be just like the first two."

Vert whimpered. Snaffle turned pale. Team Leader Flint opened her mouth to ask what was wrong but suddenly there was no time. Midge bobbed up onto her toes again.

"The deliveries are here!" she cried.

A trainee Dream Chef stepped up onto the walkway, carrying two dream boxes. She slotted them into the holders on the backs of Vert's and Snaffle's dreamskoots and then turned to leave.

"Just a minute," said Team Leader Flint, holding up her hand. "Are you sure these are the correct deliveries? The specially selected ones?"

"The Head Dream Chef picked them out himself. In person," said the trainee chef, in awed tones.

"Good. Thank Motza for me," said Team Leader Flint, waving the chef away.

Skree … skree … skree…

Team Leader Flint winced as a metallic scraping sound cut through the noise of the Dream Centre.

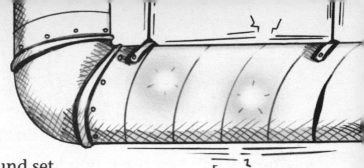

The sound set
her teeth on edge. She looked up.
A ventilation pipe stretched across the
roof space above her head. As she
watched the pipe, it gave a shudder.

Skree ... skree...

Team Leader Flint frowned. One of
the support brackets must be loose.
She made a note on her clipboard. She
would tell maintenance to get it fixed,
but first she had a group of nervous
trainees to deal with. "To your
dreamskoots!" she ordered, clapping her
hands together. "It's time to launch!"

Lying in the dust and fluff of the
ventilation pipe, Skree let out the breath
he had been holding. For a moment he
thought he had been discovered, but

Team Leader
Flint had looked right at
the pipe without realizing what
was hidden inside. Skree allowed himself
a proud smile. He could travel to every
corner of the Dream Centre without
being seen. He knew all the secret ways
and hidden places. He could slide
behind walls and crouch under floors,
watching and listening. "I know you're
not as tough as you like to act," Skree
hissed quietly, watching Team Leader
Flint's stern face through a slit he had
cut in the side of the pipe. "You really
care about your trainees. Especially little
Midge. You have a real soft spot for her,
don't you."

He shifted in the pipe until he could
see Midge through the slit. His face

twisted into a snarl. He hated all
Dream Fetchers, but he particularly
hated Midge. She had once destroyed
something of his without a second
thought. Now it was time to destroy her –
and the rest of her team. Skree could not
believe they had survived their first two
daydream deliveries. *This* time he had
made sure they would not be coming
back.

*   *   *

Vert gave a gasp of relief as he shot out
of the gateway into Earthside. His new
goggles were still working. A solid road
stretched in front of him, even though
the town was far below. He tried twirling
his dreamskoot around. The road twirled
too. Vert nodded happily. He did not feel
the slightest bit dizzy. Behind him,
Harley laughed.

"Nice flying, Vert!" she cried into his
earpiece.

"I'm not flying. I'm driving," Vert said.
"Now, let's see where this road is going."
He activated his control panel screens.
As he waited for his delivery details to
appear, he began to feel nervous. They
had all been shocked at how dangerous
Midge and Harley's daydream deliveries
had been, but they had said nothing
to Team Leader Flint. How could they

complain when Motza was giving them the easiest orders of the day? Vert gripped his handlebars more tightly. If other trainees could survive their first daydream shift, so could he. Especially now that he had the goggles.

"What have we got?" Harley asked.

Vert read out his delivery details. "Tom. A ten-year-old boy. His location is a shop storeroom. That's good, isn't it?"

"It sure is," said Harley. "There won't be any other humans in the back of a shop. All the customers stay in the front."

"What a relief," said Vert, heading for the rooftops below. "A nice quiet daydream delivery, just like Motza promised."

"Bor-ing!" sang Harley.

Vert was feeling good as he followed his own personal road all the way down to the narrow street marked on his map screen. He was beginning to think that maybe, just maybe, he could make it as a Dream Fetcher after all. The goggles had solved his fear of flying. If he could pass this one, final test, Team Leader Flint might allow him to graduate. As he skimmed along just above the roof guttering, Vert imagined the graduation ceremony. Team Leader Flint would read out his name. He would step forward and salute. His mum would cry. His dad would smile proudly and say –

"Wake up!"

Vert jumped. "Pardon?"

Harley sighed. "I said, which one is Tom's shop?"

Vert looked at the flashing red dot on his screen. "It's a bit further down on the other side," he replied.

"What's it called?" asked Harley.

"Scales."

"Hmm. Sounds like a music shop."

"Really?"

"Yeah. You know. Scales. *Do, re, mi, fa, so, la, ti, do!*" Harley sang.

Vert imagined a dim, quiet place with shelves full of violins and sheet music. "Good," he said. "A music shop sounds nice and peaceful."

"You mean boring," Harley grumbled.

Vert flew along, reading the shop names as he went. There was a flower shop called Petals, a bookshop called Brain Food and a hairdresser called Fringe Benefits. "There it is!" he said, spotting the next shop name. "Scales."

"Go on, then," Harley yawned. "Check it out."

Vert peered over the guttering into the street below. It was full of humans but they all had their heads down. He checked the rooftops for birds.

"All clear," he said, zipping across the street and hopping over the shop roof.

There was a small walled yard at the back of the shop. Vert checked for humans, dogs or cats. The yard was empty. "All clear," he said again.

"Yeah, yeah," Harley yawned. "Get on with it."

Vert lowered his dreamskoot into the yard. He checked the back door. It was shut and locked. There was no letterbox.

Vert looked for gaps. There were none. The door fitted snugly into the frame all the way round, even at the bottom.

"No way in through the door," he said. "I'll check the windows."

Harley pretended to snore. Vert smiled. There might not be enough excitement for Harley in this mission, but that was just how he liked it. He flew to the first window. It was protected by a sheet of steel mesh so fine even a fly couldn't squeeze through. Vert flew to the second window. It had the same covering of steel mesh. So did the vent for the extractor fan. There was no way in through the back of the shop.

"What are they selling in there?" he muttered, looking at the mesh-covered windows. "Solid gold recorders?"

"You know what this means?" Harley said, perking up.

"Yes. I'll have to go in through the front of the shop." Vert felt his stomach clench. This daydream delivery was not going to be quite as easy as he had hoped.

Back in the guttering at the front of the shop he took some deep, calming breaths and tried to remember what he had been taught in N.B.S. lessons. The N.B.S. course was a vital part of basic Dream Fetcher training. The letters stood for Never Be Seen. Shadow, their N.B.S. tutor, was an expert in what he liked to call "covert operations". As far as Vert could tell, that was just a fancy name for "hiding a lot". Shadow had taught them many different hiding skills, including how to get into a room full of humans without being seen. The trick was to wait for another human to open the door. The humans already in the room would look up to see who was coming in. For a few short seconds, while all the humans were looking up at the face of the new arrival, a dreamskoot could slip in through the doorway at ankle height without being seen. Shadow called it the Instant of Invisibility.

Vert gulped as he looked down at the Scales shop front. He had hoped he would never need to use the Instant of Invisibility, but it was the only way to deliver Tom's daydream. Just then, he spotted a human heading towards the shop door. This was his chance! But first he had to get down to ankle level without being seen. The street below was busy. Humans were hurrying up and down, popping in and out of shop doorways and stopping to talk to other humans. He bit his lip. If he didn't go soon, he would miss his chance – and who knew when the quiet little music shop would get another customer?

Sweat began to drip into Vert's eyes. He pulled his goggles down under his chin and wiped his face. The road under his dreamskoot disappeared. He looked down at the guttering. "Oh!" he said. "I'm sitting on it!"

"Sitting on what?" Harley asked.

"The answer. Look. There's a drainpipe right underneath us. I can get down to ankle height without being seen."

"Good thinking, Vert!" Harley said. "It's clear, too. I can see daylight at the bottom."

Vert replaced his goggles and peered out over the edge of the guttering. The human had stopped in front of the shop door and was reaching for the handle. "Hang on, Harley," he said, flicking on his headlight. "I'm going in!" He rose out of the guttering, turned his dreamskoot and shot straight into the drainpipe.

"Whoo-hoo!" Harley yelled as the tiny dreamskoot whizzed down the pipe with its headlight beam lighting the way. *Whoowhoowhoohoohoohooo...* Her voice echoed around them.

"It's a road," Vert yelped, hanging onto his handlebars for dear life. "Just a very steep road." He turned off his headlight and began to brake. An instant later he was easing his dreamskoot around the bend at the bottom of the pipe. He had done it! He peered out. He could see the customer's feet. They were stepping through the shop doorway. Before he could change his mind, Vert nipped out of the drainpipe and slipped into the shop behind the human. As soon as he was inside, he turned sharp left and hid behind a large glass case.

He held his breath and listened. The humans were greeting one another and talking about the weather. The Instant of Invisibility had worked: he had not been spotted. He took a huge, relieved breath. An instant later he slapped a hand over his nose. "Poo!"

"Exactly," Harley agreed in a muffled voice. "Poo."

The shop smelled. It smelled of leaf mould and hot, damp soil. It smelled of straw. It smelled of living things. "What *is* this place?" Vert whispered.

"Dunno," Harley said. "But I know that it isn't—"

"A music shop," Vert finished. He looked at the glass case he was hiding behind. The bottom was filled

with a thick layer of sand. Slowly he
rose up the glass side of the case until
he was above the sand. He saw a dead
branch. He saw a pile of stones. He saw
something coiled like a bicycle tyre
around the stones. He leant closer. The
tyre shot towards him. Suddenly it had
a pink, ribbed
mouth full
of fangs.

THUD!

The bicycle
tyre hit the
glass right
in front of
Vert's face.
Except it
wasn't a tyre.
It was a –

"Snake!" he
screamed. He

yanked his dreamskoot away from the tank and nearly slammed into the wall.

"Calm down, Vert!" Harley yelled. "It's in a tank!"

Vert turned his dreamskoot back to face the snake. He could hear it hissing as it slid down the glass wall. It coiled around the stones again. A forked tongue tested the air then disappeared. The snake went back to looking like a bicycle tyre. Vert edged up to the glass and peered through into the shop beyond. There were tanks of all sizes ranked around the walls. Inside them he could see bug-eyed lizards, brightly coloured frogs, enormous hairy spiders – and snakes. Lots and lots of snakes.

"Scales," he breathed. "The shop is called Scales because it sells snakes. The mesh over all the windows isn't to stop something getting in. It's to stop

anything getting out." He shuddered.
"Horrible!"

"It's not all horrible," Harley said.
"Those little birds are pretty." She
pointed to a big cage full of budgies at
the back of the shop. "And look!" She
pointed to two open-topped enclosures
below the bird cage. "They're quite cute.
From a distance."

The nearest enclosure housed seven
fluffy kittens. The far one held five plump,
black and white puppies. They were all

very young. The kittens still had blue eyes. The puppies had short, wobbly legs.

"Very nice," said Vert, but he wasn't really paying attention. He had spotted a curtain of plastic strips just beyond the puppies' enclosure. "Look. The way through to the storeroom. Tom must be behind that curtain."

"What are you waiting for?" Harley demanded. "Let's go!"

Vert eased his dreamskoot down the gap between the shelves of glass cases and the side wall of the shop. It was a nightmare journey.

Snakes lunged at him. A frog shot out its long, sticky tongue. A huge tarantula skittered forward on eight hairy legs, snapping its mandibles together.

116

Vert knew there was a wall of glass between him and all of them, but still he flinched away from every attack. Harley, on the other hand, seemed to find it funny.

"Hah!" she laughed as the tarantula crashed into the glass wall of its tank. "Not today, fungus face!"

At last Vert was hovering behind the very last tank in the row. A short hop would take him behind the curtain and into the storeroom. He peered around the corner of the tank. Two humans were standing behind a counter, talking to the customer who had opened the door for him.

"And how's young Tom?" asked the customer. "Still dreaming of being a footballer?"

"He'll grow out of it," boomed the male human behind the counter. "He's much better off working in the shop."

"But George," the female human behind the counter said. "Tom hates snakes."

"Nonsense! He's my son! He'll get used to them if he keeps trying. He's through the back now. I sent him to feed Polly."

"Polly's still growing, then?" the customer asked.

"Oh yes," George said proudly. "Want to see a photo?"

George pulled a photograph from his shirt pocket. All three humans bent their heads together. Vert took his chance. He flew out from behind the last tank, zipped across the puppy enclosure and shot between the plastic curtain strips.

In the back room, a boy was curled up in a battered old armchair. His face was streaked with dried tears. He was asleep. "That must be Tom," Vert whispered.

"But where's Polly?" Harley asked.

Vert looked around for a pram or a buggy. There was no sign of a baby human. "I thought Polly must be Tom's baby sister," he said. "Now I'm not so sure."

"What's that in Tom's lap?" Harley whispered.

Vert flew closer. Tom was clutching a perspex box with airholes in the top. A fat white mouse sat inside the box, washing its face. "Do you think that's Polly?" Vert asked.

"No," Harley whispered. "I think the mouse was supposed to be Polly's lunch. *That's* Polly."

Vert looked where Harley was pointing. An enormous snake was coiled inside a huge glass tank. It was looking right at him. Vert shot up to the ceiling and hovered there, trembling.

"Here," said Harley, poking him in the

back with a corner of the dream box she was holding. "Make your delivery and let's get out of here."

"I'm not going down there again!" Vert wailed. "Look at the size of that!"

"It's in a tank," Harley reminded him. "It can't hurt you, however big it is."

"OK. OK, you're right," said Vert. He took the dream box and floated down to Tom. As he looked at the boy's tearstained face, he felt a twinge of sympathy. Tom had tried to do something that frightened him, just to please his mum and dad. Vert knew how that felt. "I hope you score a goal in your daydream," he whispered, dropping the dream box onto Tom's cheek.

Phut!

The dream box melted into Tom's skin and Vert turned to fly back to the curtain. An instant later he screeched to a halt in mid-air. "Harley?" he squeaked in a strangled voice.

"Yes?"

"You know what you said about the snake being in a tank?"

"Yes?"

"Well, it isn't."

"What!" Harley peered around Vert's shoulder. He felt her tense as she saw what he was seeing. They were face to face with an enormous triangular head. Polly had risen up through the feeding hatch in the top of her tank. Tom must have opened the hatch to put the mouse in and then cried himself into an exhausted sleep when he realized he couldn't bring himself to do it.

"What do we do?" Vert gulped. He could see himself reflected in the snake's black, beady eyes.

"Try moving to one side," Harley whispered. "Nice and slow."

Vert flew to the left. The snake swayed with him. He flew to the right. The snake swayed too. An orange forked tongue flickered out of its mouth. More of its body rose up out of the tank. Its scales made a rasping noise as it squeezed out

through the narrow feeding hatch.

"Forget moving slowly!" squeaked Vert, shooting up to the ceiling as fast as he could. The snake made a lunge for them and missed. Its forked tongue flickered again, testing the air. Suddenly its head swung towards the shop door. It eased further out of the feeding hatch and began to coil down onto the floor.

"The puppies!" Vert gasped. "It can smell the puppies!" He put his dreamskoot into a dive and pulled up just above Tom's head. Leaning out of the saddle,

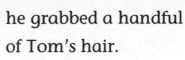

he grabbed a handful
of Tom's hair.

"What are you
doing?" Harley yelped.

"You grab some too,"
Vert ordered. "We have to
wake Tom. He has to stop the
snake before it eats the puppies!"

Harley leant down and grabbed
her own handful of hair. Vert put his
dreamskoot into reverse and they pulled
as hard as they could. Tom grunted.
His eyes opened. Quickly, they let go of
him. Vert steered his dreamskoot behind
the chair. "Come on, Tom," he said,
shakily. "Raise the alarm."

They waited for one second. Two
seconds. Three. All they could hear was
the rasping of the snake's scales as it
headed towards the puppies. Vert peered
around the side of the chair. Tom was

still sitting there, staring at the snake as it slithered past his feet. He was frozen with fear.

"Oh no!" Vert gasped. The snake had already pushed through the plastic curtain. It was sliding up the side of the open-topped puppy enclosure. Now its head was nearly at the top. Three of the puppies saw the snake. They wobbled to the far corner and squashed there together, trembling and whimpering with fear. The remaining two puppies were curled up fast asleep, directly beneath the searching head of the snake. None of the humans in the shop had seen what was happening.

Vert looked at the two sleeping puppies. Their plump, pink bellies rose and fell as they breathed. Their little paws twitched. "You're not getting those puppies," he snarled at the snake. "Not if I can help it." He looked around and spotted just what he needed. "Hang on, Harley!" he cried, flying over Tom's head towards the curtain. Tom did not notice. He was still frozen in the chair, staring at the snake. Vert slipped through the curtain and flew up to the cage of budgies. The door to the cage was held closed by a metal hook. Vert unclipped his goggles and fastened the strap around the hook. Then he rose into the air, pulling the hook up with him. The door to the budgie cage flew open and Vert dived out of sight behind the glass cases as a flock of brightly coloured birds burst out. The snake reared up, hissing at the budgies. The humans all looked towards the back of the shop.

"Tom!" the human female cried.

"Polly!" George bellowed.

"The birds!" the customer shrieked.

Everything happened very quickly
after that. George rushed over and
grabbed the snake by the neck just
as it was about to bite into one of the
puppies. Tom came out of his fear trance
and ran to help his mum catch the
budgies. The customer hurried out into
the street, waving her hands above her

head and shouting, "Get them off me!"
Vert pulled his goggles back on and flew
out after the customer. Not one human
noticed the tiny dreamskoot as it slipped
out through the doorway.

"Well done, Vert!" Harley cried as
soon as they were back at the top of the
drainpipe. "You passed! You completed
your final training mission!"

"It's no good, though," sighed Vert.
"As soon as I get back to Dreamside,
I have to quit."

"But why?" Harley gasped.

"Those puppies could have died,
Harley! All because Tom was trying to
do something that scared him, just to
please his parents. That's exactly what
I'm doing! Tom's scared of snakes. I'm
scared of flying. What if I freeze like Tom
did when we're out on a mission? I can't
risk that. If you, or Midge, or Snaffle died

because of me…" Vert stopped and shook his head. "No. I can't be a Dream Fetcher. I must give it up."

"But you have the goggles now!"

"And if I lost or broke them? What then?"

Vert lifted his goggles and looked at Harley. She gazed back at him. He could see that she did not know what to say. When their dreamcoms crackled into life, they both jumped.

"Vert! Harley!" Snaffle shrieked into their earpieces. "Help!"

"Snaffle? What's wrong?" Vert asked.

"It's Midge!" Snaffle sobbed. "You have to save her! You have to come! Please!"

The Wasp Jar

Snaffle lifted his helmet visor and put a hand to his forehead. He thought he might be coming down with something. The oddest feeling was spreading through him. It had started when they came through the gateway to Earthside. Vert had zoomed off to make his daydream delivery, wearing his new goggles and flying as straight and true as an arrow. As Snaffle had hovered above the Earthside town, watching Vert go, a strange warm glow had begun in his stomach and spread to his chest. Now it was climbing up his neck. What was wrong with him?

"Look what you did for Vert!" Midge said into his dreamcom. "He's flying beautifully. You must be feeling so proud and happy right now."

Snaffle scowled. Was that what the feeling was? He tugged at the collar of his new uniform. It was standard issue and the material was rough and scratchy. His tailor-made uniform had shrunk after he had fallen into a fish tank on his last mission. His father had sent him the money to have another one made, but he had spent it on Vert's goggles instead. *That was stupid of me*, he thought, giving his collar another yank.

"You're truly one of the team now," said Midge,

slipping her arms around his waist and giving him a hug. The odd feeling spread right up to the roots of his hair.

"Do you mind?" he said, shrugging her off. "I'm trying to check my delivery details."

Snaffle shook his head as he looked at the screen on his dreamskoot's control panel. Why were Midge, Harley and Vert acting so pleased with him all of a sudden? It was only a lousy pair of goggles! He was beginning to wish he hadn't bothered. And what was so good about being part of a team, anyway? He was heading for the top and he didn't need three losers hanging onto his shirt-tails while he did it.

Losers.

That was what his father had called his dream team.

"Just finish your training, son," he had

advised. "Then you can drop those losers. I know a very good team who are looking for a fourth right now. They're much more our sort."

Snaffle scowled as he remembered his father's words. It was good advice. So why did he feel angry every time he thought about it?

"Go on, then. Tell me," Midge said.

Snaffle stiffened. "Tell you what?"

"Your mission," Midge giggled. "Your daydream delivery. The reason we're here in Earthside. Remember?"

"Oh. Right." Snaffle looked at his screen. "I'm making a delivery to an eight-year-old female."

"What's her name?" Midge asked.

Snaffle sighed. Who cared what the name was? "Rose. All right?"

"Pretty name," Midge said. "Where is she?"

Snaffle looked at the screen. When he saw the location, a chill curled up his spine and made him shiver. "She's at school," he whispered.

His heart was beating fast as he flew his dreamskoot towards the delivery address. He knew about schools from his Human Studies lessons. It was like Basic Training back in Dreamside. Young trainees were brought together in one building to learn all sorts of things.

Which meant the school would be full of humans.

Snaffle shivered again as he remembered the terror he had felt when he saw the crowds on the station platform during Harley's mission. So many pairs of human eyes! So much daylight! He had wanted to hide away in the darkest corner he could find. Harley had kept her promise. She had not told the others how scared he had been. Now he had to get through his own daydream shift without disgracing himself.

The school was on the edge of town, next to the sea. It was surrounded by playgrounds and sports fields. Snaffle felt a bit better as he saw that the school grounds were deserted. The humans were all inside having lessons. Perhaps he would not be so frightened of being seen if they were all concentrating on learning things.

He reached the long, low red-brick building, flew down to the first window and hovered at the top. The classroom beyond was full of young humans wearing white aprons. They were standing at big tables, chopping apples and rolling out pastry. Not one human was looking his way, but he still felt like turning around and flying straight back to Dreamside.

"Oh, look!" Midge whispered. "Aren't
they sweet? It's just like our Dream
Kitchens back home. Is Rose in there?"

Snaffle shook his head and moved
on to the next window. Inside, young
humans in shorts and T-shirts were
exercising in a big room. They were
climbing bars, swinging on ropes,

leaping over benches and balancing along narrow beams.

"Oh, look!" Midge cried. "Aren't they cute? It's just like our obstacle course back home!"

"Will you stop trying to find things in common with them?" Snaffle snapped. "They're not like us. They're humans! And they're not sweet. Or cute. They're enormous – and dangerous."

There was a pause.

"Is Rose in there?" Midge asked in a small voice.

Snaffle shook his head and moved on. The next set of windows had the blinds pulled down against the sun. He peered in through the gaps between the slats. The humans were sitting at rows of desks. An adult human was standing at the front, talking. The young humans were supposed to be listening, but quite a few of them had their heads in their hands or on the desks. They looked hot and tired.

"Oh, look!" Midge whispered. "Aren't they cu— I mean, is Rose in there?"

Snaffle nodded. He pointed to a little girl directly below them. Her arm was on the windowsill and her head was resting on her arm. She was asleep.

"You're in luck," Midge said encouragingly. "Your customer is right beside the window. And look, the top part is open."

Snaffle did not feel lucky as he steered his dreamskoot through the window. The blind was between him and the humans, but they were very close. He could hear them, breathing and sighing and shuffling their feet. As he sank down towards the windowsill, he began to shake with fear. He reached the sill and hovered there, staring at the gap under the bottom of the blind. He knew he was supposed to fly under the gap and drop the dream box onto Rose's arm, but he was frozen to the spot.

"What's the matter, Snaffle?" Midge whispered.

"I – I can't do it," Snaffle moaned. "I can't go in there."

"Why not?" Midge asked.

"Too many humans," Snaffle admitted. "Too many eyes."

"But you'll only be there for a split

second. And they're all so sleepy and hot, they won't notice a thing."

Snaffle tried to make himself move out from behind the blind. He couldn't do it. "They scare me, Midge!" he wailed.

"All right," Midge said, patting his back. "All right. Don't worry. Land on the windowsill while we work out what to do."

Snaffle set his dreamskoot down. Midge peered under the blind into the classroom. Snaffle could not look. He stared out of the window instead.

"There's a nature display set out on the windowsill right next to Rose," Midge reported. "Shells and feathers. A little pile of stones and moss. Plenty of stuff to hide behind. And there are pillars at each side of the window, so the humans in the desks behind Rose won't be able to see us. It's really not too bad at all. Have a look."

Snaffle took a quick peek. The first thing he saw was Rose's huge sleeping face. The next thing he saw was all the other humans. Row after row of them. He jerked upright again. "I can't!" he moaned. "If only it was dark … but it's so bright!" He felt his dreamskoot shudder. Midge was climbing out of the saddle behind him. He looked round at her. Midge took off her helmet and put it on the windowsill. "What are you doing!" he gasped.

"I'll be better off without the helmet," she said as she pulled his daydream delivery from the holder. "I need to have a clear view all around when I'm out there."

"Out where?" Snaffle hissed.

"I'm just going to nip under the blind and deliver this daydream for you," Midge said.

"But it's my mission!"

"Well, you got us here, didn't you? That's the hard part. Sit tight. I'll be right back."

Before he could stop her, she ducked under the bottom of the blind. "Midge! Don't!" he hissed. His own voice hissed back at him from the windowsill. He jumped and looked down. Midge's helmet was lying where she had left it. There was no way she could hear him without her dreamcom. He listened hard, trying to hear Midge's footsteps, but a small plane was buzzing around outside. What was

going on beyond the blind? He took a
deep breath and bent down to look.

Midge was crouched behind a jam

 jar full of feathers.
Snaffle watched her
peer around the side
of the jar and then
sprint across to a
pile of stones and
moss. Rose's bare
arm was only inches
from the stones.
Snaffle held his
breath. Midge stuck
her head above the pile of stones for
a quick look before running out and
throwing the dream box onto Rose's arm.

The dream box landed perfectly.
Snaffle listened for the *phut* as it melted
away into Rose's skin, but all he could
hear was the buzzing plane. It was much

louder now. It sounded very close.

He looked up and stuffed his knuckles into his mouth to stop a scream. The buzzing noise wasn't a plane. A huge wasp was blundering against the inside of the window, directly above his head.

Snaffle stared at the wasp. Apart from the bright yellow stripes on its lower body, it was completely black. It had black feelers, black bulging eyes, six black spiky legs and a long black curved sting with a clear drop of venom glistening on the point. The wasp looked powerful, dangerous and very angry as it battered against the window glass. All Snaffle could think about was getting away from it.

He took off from the windowsill and rose up into the air. That was a mistake. The wasp came straight for him. The buzzing seemed as a loud as a chainsaw. Snaffle ducked. The wasp crashed against his helmet, backed off and then came in for a second attack.

Snaffle dodged and turned in the air. His dreamskoot's steering felt slow and clumsy as he twisted to avoid the deadly sting. The wasp danced around him, launching attack after furious attack.

"Snaffle!" Midge cried from below.

Snaffle faltered. The wasp jabbed
its stinger towards him. He forced
his dreamskoot into a backwards
somersault. When he levelled out again,
the wasp was heading for Midge. "Run!"
Snaffle screamed.

Midge dodged under the blind again.
The wasp zoomed after her. Snaffle
brought his dreamskoot back down to
the sill and bent to look under the blind.
Midge had squeezed into a tiny space
under the pile of stones and moss next to
Rose's head. The wasp was hovering
above the stones, making angry jabs at
her hiding place.

Snaffle relaxed a little. The wasp
couldn't reach Midge under the stones.
All they had to do was to wait until it
flew away, then Midge could scurry back
to the dreamskoot and they could both
leave this horrible windowsill behind.

The wasp flew close to Rose's head as it circled the stones, buzzing furiously. Rose opened her eyes. She saw the wasp and sat up. Snaffle froze. He knew that many humans were afraid of wasps. If Rose began to scream or flap, all the other humans would turn to look, and Midge might be discovered. Snaffle bit his lip and waited to see what Rose would do. She didn't scream or flap. She did something far worse. She grabbed the jam jar, turned it upside-down and emptied out the feathers. Then she rammed the jar down over the pile of stones, trapping the wasp – and Midge – inside.

Snaffle let out an anguished groan. Midge would not survive in the jar for long. Even if she managed to avoid the wasp, she couldn't avoid the sun. It was shining through the gap under the

blind, directly onto the glass. Very soon the temperature inside the jar would become unbearable. The wasp began to throw itself against the glass. Rose rested her head on the windowsill and watched the wasp sleepily for a few seconds before her eyes closed again.

As soon as Snaffle was sure Rose had gone back to sleep, he scrambled from his dreamskoot. Before he could lose his nerve, he scurried out from behind the blind and skidded across to the jar, grabbing one of the feathers as he went. Panting with fear, he stuck the pointed end of the feather's quill under the rim of the jar. Trying not to think about the rows of humans all around him, he pushed down on the quill as hard as he could. If he could lever the jar up high enough, Midge might be able to crawl out. Midge saw what he was doing. She

rolled out from under the stone, stuck
her fingers under the rim of the jar and
tried to help him lift.

The jar wouldn't move, however much
they strained. Finally Midge fell back
and sat on the moss, gasping with
exhaustion and rubbing at her sore
fingers. She was very flushed, her ears
were drooping and her hair hung in
limp strands. She staggered to her feet,

pressed her hands against the glass and looked out at Snaffle. He gazed back at her. Slowly, hopelessly, Midge shook her head. A tear trickled down her cheek. Snaffle felt his throat close up.

Just then, the wasp crashed against the side of the jar just above Midge's head. She ran, scrambling away over the stones. The wasp went after her. Snaffle grabbed the quill and pushed down with all his remaining strength. The jar shifted. Lifted. His arms were trembling with effort. He saw Midge scrambling towards him, heading for the narrow gap he had created. He pressed down harder, determined to hold on. Midge flung herself to the ground and began to roll under the rim.

Snap!

The quill broke in half. The rim of the jar thudded down. Midge pulled back just in time. The jar rattled against the windowsill as the rim settled back into place.

Rose began to stir. Her eyes flickered open. Snaffle did the only thing he could. He turned and ran for his hiding place behind the blind. As soon as he reached his dreamskoot, he looked back. Midge had squeezed herself under the stones again. The wasp circled above her. The inside of the jar shimmered with heat.

Snaffle pressed the alarm button on his dreamskoot's control panel. When the alarm button was activated, a siren sounded back in the Dream Centre. The siren was a signal that a Dream Fetcher was in serious trouble. Snaffle knew that Dreamside Search and Rescue would already be scrambling for their skoots. He also knew that they would arrive too late to save Midge. It would take them at least fifteen minutes to find the school. By then, Midge would have been stung by the wasp or overcome with heat exhaustion. Snaffle picked up Midge's helmet and cradled it against his chest. He began to sob. What could he do on his own? His eyes widened. He had suddenly remembered that he was not alone at all.

Quickly he scrambled back into the saddle of his dreamskoot and brought up a map of the Earthside town on his screen. A flashing dot marked Vert and Harley's position. Snaffle narrowed his eyes, calculating the distance. They were less than a minute away! Snaffle opened the outside channel on his dreamcom and sent out a cry for help.

Vert and Harley were by his side even faster than he had hoped.

"Where is she?" Harley demanded as
Vert brought his dreamskoot in to land
on the windowsill.

Wordlessly Snaffle pointed to the
jam jar. The wasp was still blundering
against the glass. Rose was sitting with
her chin propped in her hands, watching
it. Midge was under the stone with her

face turned away from the hot sun.
She was not moving. The glass was
beginning to steam up.

Vert and Harley gazed at the scene
through the slats of the blind. Snaffle
watched them hopefully. He couldn't see
a way to rescue Midge, but perhaps they
would come up with something he had
not thought of.

"Are you sure Midge is unconscious?"
Harley asked. "Have you tried speaking
to her?"

Snaffle held up Midge's helmet. Harley
and Vert looked at it and then back to
the jar. Their faces were grim. Snaffle's
shoulders sagged. He could feel the last
bit of hope draining out of him.

"Fire alarm!" Harley cried suddenly.
Snaffle looked up.

"If we set off the fire alarm, all the
humans will leave the classroom and we

can get Midge out of the jar," Harley said. "Come on, Vert! Get moving."

"Hang on," said Vert. "Don't you have to break the glass on the front of the little box?"

"We're not bothering with that," Harley snapped. "There'll be a master button in the school office, for when they need to test the alarm. We can just press that. One good nudge with the nose of your dreamskoot should do it."

"We passed the office on our way in," Vert said. "The window was open."

"Let's go!" Harley cried. "Snaffle, you stay here and keep an eye on Midge."

Vert took off and zoomed out of the window. Snaffle waited on the sill. And waited. He watched Midge, hoping to see a movement. She was completely still.

"Come on," Snaffle pleaded.

KER-LANG-LANG-LANG-LANG!!!

The alarm
was so loud,
it made the
windows rattle.
Snaffle grabbed
onto the
handlebars of
his dreamskoot. In
the classroom, all the humans began to
stand up and file towards the door.

"You did it!" Snaffle shouted as Vert
and Harley returned. "Now for the next
stage!" The last human was barely out
of the room when Snaffle shot out from
behind the blind. He positioned his
dreamskoot near the top of the jar. Vert
pulled alongside, wrenching off his
steamed-up goggles and hanging them
over his handlebars. Behind Vert, Harley
was clutching a feather like a spear.
Together, Snaffle and Vert flew their

dreamskoots at the jar and gave it a
hard nudge. The jar tipped and then
settled back over the stones.

"Harder!" yelled Snaffle. Vert nodded.
This time they drove their dreamskoots
into the glass so hard, the shock nearly
jolted them from their saddles. The jar
tipped, hesitated and then toppled right
over. The wasp flew out.

"You go get Midge!" Harley cried to Snaffle. She took a firm grip on her feather and then tapped Vert on the shoulder. He put his head down and drove straight for the wasp.

"You think you've got a big sting?" Harley yelled, jabbing at the wasp with her feather. "Well have a taste of this!"

They chased the wasp all the way across the empty classroom and into the corridor. Snaffle left them to it. He landed beside the little pile of stones, scrambled from the saddle and crouched beside Midge. She did not move. He eased her out from under the stones. She was limp and pale. Her eyes were closed. Snaffle pulled a water bottle from the special slot on his dreamskoot.

He popped the cap and
lifted Midge so that her head
was resting in the crook of his arm.
Gently, he dribbled some water between
her lips. It dribbled out again and ran
down her chin. "Oh, Midge. I'm sorry.
Please wake up," he whispered.

Vert landed beside them. Harley
scrambled from the saddle and pulled
her mother's old kerchief from her neck.
She soaked a corner with water from
Snaffle's bottle and mopped Midge's face
with it. Vert picked up
one of the feathers
and used it as a
fan, sending

cooling air across her limp body. Still she did not move. The fire alarm stopped and silence filled the empty classroom.

"It's my fault," Snaffle cried into the silence. "Midge came out here on foot to make my delivery because I was too scared to fly out in front of all those humans. It's all my fault!" He looked up at Harley and Vert, waiting for the angry words to start. Instead, Vert and Harley both nodded.

"Of course she did," Harley said simply.

"You would have done the same for any one of us," Vert added. "That's the way it is."

Snaffle felt his eyes fill with tears. Finally he understood what a dream team was for. A tear ran down his cheek and splashed onto Midge's face.

"Euch!" Midge spluttered faintly. "Stop crying on me." Her eyes fluttered

open and she smiled up
at Snaffle.

"Midge!" Snaffle cried.
"I was so scared! I called
out Search and Rescue
and everything."

"Then you'd better
let them know I'm OK,"
Midge said, struggling into a
sitting position. She grabbed the water
bottle and took a long, long drink.

"Are you sure?" Harley said. "I mean,
you might need medical attention or
something."

"You just want Cheroot to come flying
in here like a knight on a white horse,"
Midge teased.

"Some knight he'd make, with his
tattoos and his bristly haircut," Harley
sniffed, but she was grinning as she
said it.

"Call them off," Midge ordered in a much stronger voice.

Harley nodded and spoke into her dreamcom.

"We don't need Search and Rescue," Midge continued. "We're the Dream Team. We're going to fly back to Dreamside on our own. Right?"

Snaffle stood up straight and lifted his chin. "Right!" he agreed. He scrambled onto his dreamskoot and nodded to Harley and Vert. They lifted Midge onto the saddle in front of him,

so that she was sitting with her head resting against his shoulder. Both dreamskoots lifted off and flew out of the classroom window just as the humans began pouring back in from the yard outside.

"We'd better graduate after all this!" Harley yelled as they soared across the sky towards the gateway.

"Attention, Dream Centre!" Team Leader Flint's voice boomed over the loudspeaker system. "The ceremony is about to start!"

All over the centre, work came to a halt. The Dream Chefs stopped clattering in the kitchens. The mechanics stopped testing dreamskoot engines in the garages. The windows of the Dream Traffic Control Centre were suddenly full of spectators as the controllers left their monitor screens. For a few moments, all eyes were on Midge, Vert, Harley and Snaffle as they stood in a line in front of their launch pads. Most of those eyes were friendly and smiling, but one pair of eyes burned with hatred. Skree was hidden behind an ornamental

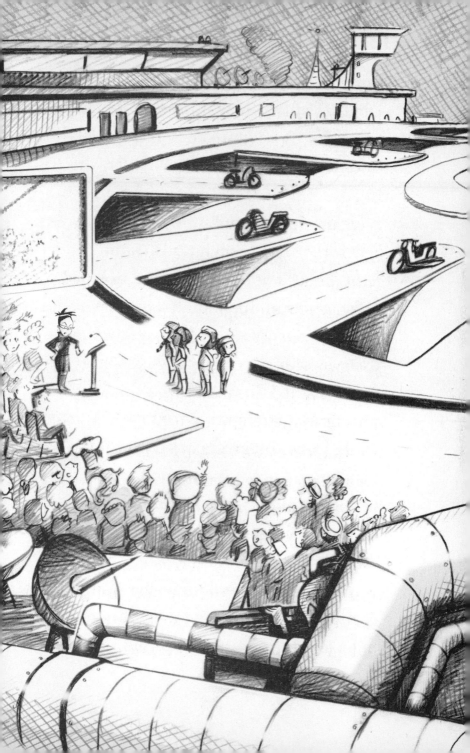

panel high up in the back wall of the Dream Centre. He was almost dancing with rage as he glared down at Midge and her team. "This isn't over yet," he hissed. "I swear I will not stop until I have destroyed you!"

Down on the launch pads, Team Leader Flint glanced at her watch and frowned. They were running late. It was the custom for a trainee dream team to go through their graduation ceremony as soon as they returned from their final mission. This time the ceremony had been delayed while Motza had rampaged through his Dream Kitchens, looking for the chef who had mixed up four easy daydream deliveries with four difficult and dangerous orders. He had not found the culprit. He was standing in the small crowd of invited guests now, managing to look both stricken and proud.

Team Leader Flint gave Motza a nod and then turned to look at Midge. She was still pale and a bit wobbly. Team Leader Flint thought about offering a chair, but Midge was standing to attention with a fiercely determined look on her face. Team Leader Flint decided to let it pass. She lowered her microphone so that only her four trainees could hear.

"Listen up, trainees," she said to them for the very last time. "Before this final mission, I wasn't sure whether to let you graduate. I thought you were never going to become a proper dream team. Today you proved me wrong. You worked together as a team under the most difficult circumstances. Well done. I'm proud of you."

Team Leader Flint smiled at them and then looked down at her boots. She cleared her throat a few times and then lifted the microphone to her mouth.

"Trainee Midge! Step forward!"

Midge marched up to Team Leader Flint and gave her smartest salute. As Team Leader Flint bent to pin on her graduation badge, Midge looked out at the crowd of guests. Her mum and dad were standing there, smiling up at her. Midge smiled back proudly. At last she was a fully qualified Dream Fetcher! With her badge in place, Midge stepped up onto the podium. She looked up at the monitor screen above the crowd. Her friend Velvet was watching the whole ceremony from The Below by cam-link. She waved at Midge and gave her a thumbs-up.

"Trainee Vert! Step forward!"

Vert stumbled up to Team Leader Flint.

"Um, boss?" he whispered, as she bent to pin on his badge. "I – I'm not sure you should let me graduate."

"But you flew beautifully today, Vert," Team Leader Flint murmured.

"Yes, but only because of these special goggles Snaffle got for me," Vert admitted.

"What goggles?" asked Team Leader Flint.

Vert reached a hand up to his neck. The goggles were not there. His eyes widened as he remembered slipping them onto his handlebars when they were at the school. He turned to look at his dreamskoot. The goggles were still hanging from his handlebars. Suddenly Vert realized that he had helped to rescue Midge and then

flown all the way home to Dreamside without them. "Oh!" he gasped, turning back to Team Leader Flint.

"Exactly," smiled Team Leader Flint, pinning on his graduation badge.

Vert stepped onto the podium next to Midge. He looked down at the crowd of guests. His mum and dad were right at the front. His mum was crying and his dad looked so proud he was nearly bursting out of his best suit jacket. Vert laughed out loud. He had made it!

"Trainee Harley! Step forward!"

Harley sauntered up to Team Leader Flint with a broad grin on her face. Team Leader Flint tutted as she bent to pin on Harley's badge. Harley looked down at the guests. Dare was standing at the back. His hair was sticking up all over the place as usual. His blue eyes sparkled as he gazed up at her. He

brought his heels
together and saluted.
Harley returned
his salute and then
touched her hand to
her neckerchief. "Mum?
Dad?" she whispered. "Are
you watching out there
somewhere? If you are, this is for you.
I love you both."

"Trainee Snaffle! Step forward."

Snaffle straightened up his
uniform and gave a crisp
salute. As Team Leader Flint
bent to pin on his graduation
badge, he saw a shadowy
figure standing on the
observation platform next to
the Dream Traffic Control
Tower. The figure moved
slightly and Snaffle caught

the gleam of medals. It was his father. Snaffle stared up at him. He knew why his father was there. He was waiting for what would come next. Snaffle swallowed hard and took his place on the podium next to the others.

"And now," Team Leader Flint boomed, "as is the tradition, each of these new graduates must decide whether they wish to remain with their dream team or be transferred." She turned to look at Midge, Harley, Vert and Snaffle. "Speak now. Do you wish to stay or leave?"

"Stay!" Midge called in a clear, high voice.

"Stay!" Vert squeaked nervously.

"Stay," drawled Harley with a grin.

Snaffle hesitated. He looked up at his father. He looked at Midge, Vert and Harley. He made his decision.

"Stay!" he cried. When he looked up
at the observation platform again, the
shadowy figure had disappeared. Snaffle
was surprised to discover that he did not
mind very much.

"Then I declare you to be a dream
team!" Team Leader Flint boomed.

"Stay true to one another, for you will never find better friends!"

The whole Dream Centre erupted into cheers. Every dreamskoot on the launch pads rose into the air and dipped their wings in a salute. Midge, Vert, Harley and Snaffle crowded together and hugged one another. They were the Dream Team at last.